Tales from Ashen

Tales from Ashen Falls by Paul S. Lavender

All the characters in this book are fictitious, and any resemblance to persons, living or dead, is purely coincidental.

Copyright by the author of this book. The book retains sole copyright to his or her contributions to this book.

Cover Art by Betibup33 and more can be found at http//thebookcoverdesigner.com/designers/betibup33/

Tales from Ashen Falls

Introduction

I had finished (to a point) The Eighth God and had had ten copies printed off to give to family and friends so that they could feed back to me.

One of the lucky (or not!) ones was David N. Humphrey, author of Knight of Coins and Ten of Swords.

One of the things he liked was Pock and Cock and thought that they should have their own spin-off book.

And so I wrote Tales from Ashen Falls, which while not exclusively about Pock and Cock does have them in three of the four stories. They also return in the second of The Orcslayer books, The Sect of Seven.

The book gives a good insight into how The Eighth God reads and has some of the main characters from that book in it as well. So if you enjoy these, then you should enjoy The Eighth God.

Paul S. Lavender
2016

Tales from Ashen Falls

Table of contents

Melress and The Fading Man........................5
The Dove's Head 29
Melress Investigates 51
The Scarecrow...69

Tales from Ashen Falls

Melress and The Fading Man

Tales from Ashen Falls

What is the fading man?
You ask as you speed by,
A thing with teeth, you don't want to meet,
Is my hurriedly shouted reply.

Where lives the fading man?
Your next question is a yell.
In a dark cave, on a bed of bones,
A child's idea of hell.

Why is the fading man?
You shout as you disappear inside.
To keep you sweet, your parents keep
Letting him out to fly.

Children's Rhyme

Tales from Ashen Falls

Melress sat under the old oakenwood tree; he often came here when he was at his lowest, and he was always low at this time of year.

His birthday.

Somewhere in the house, his mother would be bossing the servants around, making preparations for the feast that would be served tonight.

As usual, his father wouldn't be there, just lots of adults Melress would hardly know; maybe his cousin Alfrick would come, but then hadn't his mother said that he had joined the army?

He missed his dad and wished he could be here, but his father had been recalled to court by King Eionnen and had then had swiftly gone to the orc lands as ambassador, his mother receiving a letter from the King two days later.

His mother had cried herself to sleep that night; the letter crumpled in her hand. As a human woman with a half-elven child, she was extremely lucky to have received any letter at all. Elves of any station considered themselves to be above humans and any bastard progeny, luckily half-elves didn't happen too often, but it did seem to be becoming more common as human women were more fertile and were more numerous than their elven counterparts.

Melress had asked his mother what the letter had said, but she just cried again and hugged him to her bosom. He had found it all rather embarrassing.

He would have to leave the shelter of the Oakwood tree soon, it was getting dark, and the odd drop of rain was striking the leaves above him. Sure enough, from the direction of the house, his mother's voice drifted to him.

Melress...

That voice was closer, more masculine.

Melress...

There it was again, intrigued Melress headed further into the garden, even as he knew he should be heading back to the house. He found the source soon enough. An unfamiliar man sat on a rock not far from where he had been hiding.

Melress wasn't scared; he was after all seven human years old, had his dagger and was in a garden surrounded by eight feet high walls.

Tales from Ashen Falls

The man had long dark blond hair that hung over a lined forehead, between some of the strands the man's ice blue eyes shone. He wore a tunic and trousers. A black belt was around his waist with a pouch hanging from it.

Melress couldn't see any weapons, but approached the man cautiously, "Who are you?"

His voice sounded thin and reedy even to himself, and he added, "Sir?"

The man smiled. Melress shivered, it wasn't a pleasant smile. He turned to run.

The man's voice came just before arms grabbed him, "Too late, boy, far too late."

Suddenly he was tucked under the man's arm, and then the man was running. He bounded over the wall as if it was only a foot high. Houses flashed past as Melress was jostled and jolted along, he opened his mouth to shout for help, but the words wouldn't come out.

It didn't take the man long to leave Ashen Falls behind, and soon they were running through trees. Melress was totally confused as to where he was, he spent most of his life at home, with tutors coming to him,

Tales from Ashen Falls

to educate and train him.
    The man kept running, his breathing normal, unaware that inhuman eyes were following along behind.

Tales from Ashen Falls

Alwine Melbrugess cursed her son even as she shouted his name again. Where was the boy? She didn't need this, what with her husband away and tonight's festivities. Melress was growing so fast, soon as per her husband's wishes, he would be sent away to the army, where his training would begin in earnest. Then she would be alone.

Most of her husband's people looked down at her and wouldn't even speak to her, even though they would take her money every week. Melress had had it worse, but she had managed to pay for three humans and replace the sour faced elves. One of the humans came through the open door, buckling on a plain Longwood as he did so. "Problem?"

Alwine looked at the man, so muscular and tough, if she weren't married, she would gladly be seen walking arm in arm down the street with this man, but then she mused, she didn't even know if Brett was his first or last name.

"I don't know Brett; he should have come back by now!" She was beginning to panic, but their time together was running out, her husband had bought Melress a commission in the army. He would leave for

the garrison town of Riverview in two weeks.
"Go back inside ma'am, the rain's gettin' heavier. I'll go and find the lad."
She sighed and was about to protest when the rain suddenly picked up and screeching in shock at the cold droplets; she rushed indoors.

Tales from Ashen Falls

Brett smiled as his boss ran inside, it was a smile that seemed to reflect sadness because he knew how she felt about him. If he were honest with himself he would give his right arm - well no, his left one - he held his sword in his right to be with Alwine. She was beautiful and graceful, but it could never be they swam in different circles.

With a sigh, he strode off into the rain. He knew Melress liked to sit under the Oakwood tree, and that's where he started his search for the lad. As he approached the tree, he started casting a spell to make Melress's tracks glow. He just hoped that the rain wouldn't get any worse, or the spell would fail.

He followed the footprints until they suddenly disappeared. He swore to himself as he scanned the ground in front of him, it was then that he noticed a half a print in the ground, this one larger, a man's. Brett re-cast the spell on the new print and started to follow the trail.

Tales from Ashen Falls

Caw had been sitting on a branch when the man had come running through with a very scared looking boy tucked under one arm. He was sure the child was trying to scream, but his mouth was just opening and closing like a fishes. Still, Caw was a nosey bastard, and that was, in his opinion, what made him special. He didn't want to just hang out with the other Ravens; he wanted to see the world and experience new things.

That was why he followed the pair, lifting off into the air without a sound. Normally, he would be roosting with the other day birds, but Caw had always been able to see in the dark, none of the elder birds knew why it should be so.

Caw continued to follow the pair until they went into a cave. Frustrated Caw circled above the entrance a few times, then after taking a deep breath plunged into the cave.

Tales from Ashen Falls

The man slowed down as they entered the cave, he avoided the stalagmites and stalactites that sprung up in clusters, caused by the water that dripped through the roof of the cavern. While the entrance to the cave had been small, it had soon opened up into a large cavern. The man continued to walk on, and Melress could see at the back of the cavern another tunnel, with a torch in a sconce halfway down.

    Once into this tunnel, the man turned and pulled a lever sticking out of one of the walls. The lever was old and rusty, but where it entered the mechanism, it had been well oiled. A lattice of wood slid across the tunnel. The man set Melress down. Looking at the boy, he licked his lips slightly, "Scream if you want boy, no one will hear you."

    Melress looked at the man, he felt strangely relaxed and not in the least bit scared. His heart he knew should be racing, after all, he had just been snatched by a nursery rhyme character.

    "What do you want from me, sir?"

    "Tell me, boy, what do you know about The Fading Man?"

    "Ha, it's a rhyme, a story to scare naughty boys and girls. Nothing more."

Tales from Ashen Falls

As Melress was speaking, the man's features were changing, becoming almost bat-like, beady eyes stared at Melress, and a tongue flicked out.

Melress turned and ran down the corridor.

The Fading Man slowly walked forwards, "Run, run little boy, you will taste sweeter when I catch you."

Melress was lucky that half-elves had some darkness vision, not as much as a full elf would, but he would have an advantage that a human child wouldn't in the dark. He also remembered that he still had his dagger in its sheath, as he ran he drew the small blade.

He could hear the man behind him; he was yelling insults at the boy, trying to scare him, but Melress kept running down the corridor. Soon he was in another, smaller cavern, a straw mat lay in the far corner, at the opposite side lay a pile of children's garments and toys. Next to the pile sat three cages, just big enough to hold a smallish child, two of the cages were empty. A girl sat crossed legged in the other, she had her back hunched and was quietly sobbing.

Melress ran over to the cage. The girl

jumped as she noticed the half-elf for the first time. He just had time to cut the rope that was keeping the door closed when the man came in.

"Ah, there you are boy, I don't know your name, so I think I'll just call you supper."

Melress threw his dagger at the creature as it advanced, the creature swatted the blade contemptuously away to land near the three cages.

"Come to me boy; you can't escape. I promise to make your death swift. Come."

"But I haven't been naughty, why are you doing this!"

"You were hiding from your mother; you were scaring her, with your father away she needs you to be the strong one. Shall I go on?"

"But you're being naughty too! You can't go around just eating children willy-nilly, it's not right!"

The creature stopped and cocked his head to one side. "Let me tell you something Supper. Once I was a mighty warrior, fabled throughout the land, I was mightier that my three brothers and they were mighty too!"

"That's a lot of might in my opinion!"

"Aye, well. It wasn't enough for my

brothers, and one night they attacked me, and I had to kill all three. My mother ran to their bodies and wept over her sons, and then she cursed me. It wasn't my fault her sons were dead, and yet I was cast out from our village, and as I walked the curse took hold and so now I am as you see me. I am what I am and like the snake or the crocodile I cannot change."

    Melress could feel himself beginning to relax as the creature spoke, alluring tones wiping away the young boy's fears.

    He took a step forward, and suddenly the creature before him was screaming as a large black shape flew at its face. Talons raked across the creature's eyes, blood dripping down to confuse it momentarily. The creature flailed its arms, and a lucky swipe sent the bird spinning.

    But the bird had blinded the creature temporarily, and as it stood wiping the blood from its eyes, the girl had opened the cage door and picked up the dagger.

Tales from Ashen Falls

Brett had worked his way through the forest that preceded the entrance to the cave. He had been lucky, as the trees had allowed his tracking spell to work without a hitch, keeping the majority of the rain off the route the footprints had taken. The spell had used little energy, and he had only aged a week, a rest and a cup of tea would have back to normal. He just hoped that he didn't have to use too much power today, his days as a Battle Mage were long gone and he was getting old - or so his joints told him on cold days.

As he approached the entrance to the cave, he unsheathed his long sword. Three runes glowed along its steel blade, the blue light giving Brett something to see by, he could have used more illumination but was hesitant to use the energy. With a sinking feeling in his heart, he entered the dark portal.

Even though he was worried about the boy, he advanced slowly and carefully through the cavern, following the faintly glowing footprints.

He came to a point where the footprints went into the rock face in front of him. Cursing under his breath, he started to

Tales from Ashen Falls

look for a mechanism to open the secret door.

Tales from Ashen Falls

Melress edged his way crab-like toward the still form of the bird. He wondered why it had come to his aid; perhaps the gods did look on half-elves sometimes. As he edged closer, he risked a glance at the body, but he couldn't tell if the bird was alive or not. He bent down to feel if the bird was still warm, as he did so three things happened at once.

The first thing was that the man-creature cleared its eyes, which then bored into the half-elf before him. The creature was just about to step forward when the girl thrust Melress's dagger up into the creature's groin. The creature shrieked, which caused Melress to step back, his foot brushing an outstretched wing of the bird.

Melress's hair stood up, and the bird's eyes widened in shock as electricity flew from the half-elf towards the hilt of the dagger. As the electricity sent shock after shock into the creature, the girl was flung away.

The creature screamed more and more as it's clothing caught fire, and then the creature itself lit up like a candle, flesh melting off his face and limbs to drip into puddles on the cave floor. The smell of burning meat hit the two children, and they put hands over noses to stop the worst of the stench.

Caw struggled to his claws with a grain as the boy stooped down and picked him up.

"Huh, won't be much to eat of him not so much as a juicy eyeball."

The boy looked in wonder at the bird in his arms, "That was the worst thing I have ever heard!"

"You can understand me?"

"Yes, is that a problem?"

"Well, it could be, but we can discuss that later. Now, I think you, me and that little lady over there had better get out of here; I'm not really a cave person."

Melress ran over to the girl, as he did so the bird took flight from his hands. Melress grabbed the girl with one of his now free hands and pulled towards the tunnel. They stopped as they were about to enter it and looked back, all they could see was a smoking pile of gloop on the floor. Taking the girl by the hand, they walked quickly up the tunnel.

Tales from Ashen Falls

Brett was starting to panic, nowhere could he find a switch or lever to open the secret door, there had to be some magic protecting it. He started to cast a spell, hoping that he knew roughly where a switch would be located.

Before he could cast it, however, the rock surface began to slide out of the way. Brett held his sword hilt tighter as a figure emerged from the tunnel beyond. The runes on the blade shone brighter and lit up Melress, who had a large raven sat on his head and was leading a little girl by the hand.

Brett looked past the group, "Where's the creature?"

Melress and the girl both said, "Dead" at the same time.

"Dead? I doubt that, little ones. We may just have enough time to get out of here before it comes looking for you. Now let's go!"

The three of them headed out of the cave; Brett walked in front, and the two children followed behind.

When they left the cave, the little girl piped up, "Where are we? Who are you? What was that creature?"

Brett smiled. "Not now little one, we

need to keep moving, time enough for questions and answers when we get to young Melress's home."

"You should be addressing me as your highness, or that's what my tutors tell me is the correct way to talk to a princess."

Brett stopped walking so fast that Melress walked into the back of him. "What is your name, little one, err your highness?"

"Princess Beatrice Alberta Fiona Hamerband."

"Oh...well Princess, at the moment, I am the only person keeping you safe, so lose the haughty air and do as I say!"

The Princess ran a finger through her hair, and Melress noticed that the tips were slightly pointed like his own.

She's a half-elf too! He thought to himself.

The three walked on and as they walked Melress told Brett about what had happened after he had been abducted. Once or twice Brett would ask a question, especially when Melress got to the part about the raven.

The raven opened its beak, "Caw, my name is Caw, and it would seem I am now your familiar, Melress."

Tales from Ashen Falls

Princess Beatrice looked at the bird, "Why is he making all that awful noise?"

"He's telling those that can understand him his name, isn't that right Caw?"

Caw looked at the man known as Brett, "Battle Mage. I know you now..."

"Yes, well this isn't about me, Caw. I thank the gods that you have found each other, although the gods know what his mother and father will say."

The boy piped up, "What's going on? Why can we understand Caw when the Princess can't."

Brett looked at the boy, "Basically; I am, or rather was a Battle Mage. I'm now retired - you, however, are about to become a Battle Mage. Your father had commissioned you into the army, but now your innate magic has been awakened you won't be allowed. You'll be commissioned into the Battle Mages within a week..."

"A week!"

"...But you will be based here in Ashen Falls so that you will get to see your parents now and again."

"But...But I'm only seven. It's my birthday today. I don't want to go! I won't

Tales from Ashen Falls

go!"
"Be careful Melress, you might summon the Fading Man again!"
Melress snapped his mouth shut and didn't say another word all the way home.

Tales from Ashen Falls

Trevor stood under the first span of the bridge crossing the River Rush, the rusty blade of his knife scraped along the stonework. He tried to pull the stone, and it wiggled loose a little bit.

He grinned as he jammed the blade into the cement again.

An arm grabbed hold of his waist, while a hand put pressure on the hand holding the knife causing him to drop it. A voice spoke from behind him, 'Never let it be said that The Fading Man can't learn from failure.'

Suddenly Trevor found himself moving at a fast rate, leaving behind a rusty knife and a lingering scream.

In the village of Hardstone, a man stared into a bowl of water as the images faded. Well, he mused, he had started the ball rolling, and it was all down to the Gods now.

Oh, wait.

Tales from Ashen Falls

Tales from Ashen Falls

The Dove's Head

The Dove's Head Inn sits on the corner of Main Street and Priests Row in the city of Ashen Falls. It has a strange shape for an Inn, being more of an L shape rather than the typical rectangle.

The Inn's name was derived not from the bird but the illustrious thief of the same name.

The Dove was caught in the act of stealing a gold and emerald necklace from a local merchant. A present it was said for his mistress who was a third of his age. As The Dove had tried to make his escape with the ill-gotten gains he had been trapped by the city watch at the intersection of the two streets.

The city watch had been the laughing stock of the common people due to their failures in capturing the Thief, and it was said that by the time they had finished the only thing recognisable was the head. This was mostly due to it having been neatly chopped off early on in the proceedings.

Tales from Ashen Falls

Plus, there was a bounty on the head of one hundred Gold Heads, a not inconsiderable amount back in those days.

So the inn had changed its name from the rather mundane Ashen Falls Inn to the far more violent (in the owner's opinion) The Doves Head Inn.

Inside the Inn apart from the usual tables and chairs and of course bar with its various liquors on display there sits a wooden box with a glass front. Inside is the preserved remains of *THE* Dove's head; the mouth is slightly open, and the eyes slightly closed giving it the look of someone who has just woken up.

Ashen Falls is a city famous for two things. The first is the exquisite glassware that is made from the extinct volcano that towers over the City. The second is that it is the headquarters of the Battle Mages, an ancient order of spellcasting warriors.

The Inn has two bouncers standing outside on either side of the entrance. The man on the left is noticeable for all the pock marks that cover his face. Humourlessly, the citizens of Ashen Falls have taken to calling the man Pock.

Tales from Ashen Falls

His real name is Albert, but if you were to use it, Pock would feel obliged to pull your arms out of their sockets and beat you to death with them.

On the other side of the entrance stood his brother Cock. Now let us be clear that Cock did not get his name because he has a foot-long sub. No, Cock keeps chickens in the hovel that the two brothers called home.

The two brothers could almost be twins. Both men have short cut black hair and coal black eyes. However, Cock is two years younger and stands slightly taller than his six feet two-inch brother.

Pock and Cock are usually kept pretty busy as the bouncers of The Doves Head Inn. They also have to protect it from more than the usual drunks and thieves what with the battle mages and the adventurers on route to the old cities beyond the Orc Lands.

Pock shifted his weight even as he stretched his arms out. As the man approached, he cracked his knuckles and smiled his best *'I could easily break you'* look.

Cock watched cautiously as the approaching man looked at his Brother.

Tales from Ashen Falls

The man's eyes had narrowed slightly, but that was the only reaction he made.

The two brothers took a good look at the man, scanning him from top to bottom and back again.

The man was wearing black boots, black trousers and an off-white silk shirt. The shirt had yellow thread work on the collar and cuffs. It probably would have been an expensive item, but it was beginning to have seen better days.

Strangely, for Ashen Falls, the man had ginger hair which was tightly curled and down the sides of his face were mutton chop sideburns. Ginger hair was very rare in Ashen Falls, and this alone marked the man out as probably being a visitor to the City.

The two bouncers decided it was unlikely that the man was a battle mage as they usually wore a small badge with their insignia on it. This was because the insignia, more often than not, kept most of the trouble caused by over enthusiastic drunks and thieves away.

The man had a slight smile on his face as he walked past the two bouncers which did nothing to ease Pock and Cocks minds but the man wasn't doing anything that they could stop him from entering the Inn.

Time passed uneventfully for the two bouncers, and soon they found themselves inside the inn chasing the last of the regulars out onto the street.

Once the Inn had been cleared the two brothers went over to one of the tables around the corner of the L, where the manager of the inn was already sitting. A jug of cold ale and two full mugs sat in the middle of the table, and the manager had a third mug of the dark foamy liquid in his right hand.

The manager had earned himself the moniker of Duke during his short tenure of the inn. No one knew what had happened to the old manager, and no one cared as he had been a total wanker.

And he had kept on increasing the prices ever so slightly, which never went down well.

Pock, closely followed by Cock, sat down and reached for one of the remaining mugs. Then Pock gave a contented sigh as the liquid slid down towards his bladder, "That is a nice drop, which one is it?"

Tales from Ashen Falls

Duke smiled, "It's new Pock. I heard about it from a reliable source; it's called Boars Piss."

Cock was swilling a second mouthful around and nodding sagely.

"Might have to get some for home." Pock took another sip.

"Been a quiet night tonight hasn't it?" Duke said into the ale fed silence.

"Aye.' Said Pock and Cock in unison.

Then Pock shifted on his seat and let out a tremendous fart, "Cut the chit chat Duke and get the cards dealt."

Duke pulled some tattered cards out of his shirt pocket even as the other arm started to waft the smell of Pock's fart about.

"What the fuck have you been eating?"

Pock started to answer, but Duke interrupted, "No, don't bother. It stinks whatever the fuck it was."

The three men sat and played a few hands of cards in companionable silence. Now and then one of them would lift a bum cheek and let off a stinker, and the other two would windmill their arms until the air was breathable again.

Tales from Ashen Falls

Copper Heads changed hands as the games finished and for once it looked as if Duke was in favour with the God of Luck. The human God of Luck was known as Luck and usually was proceeded with an expletive like, 'That was fucking Lucky!' or 'I could really do with some sodding Luck!'

Cock was frowning even as he looked down at the cards he had been given when the lantern that was the only source of light in the inn at the time went out.

The smell of rot followed hard on the heels of the darkness.

Pock and Cock dropped down to the floor as a buzzing noise started to get louder and louder. Then the buzzing noise began to recede even as there was the sound of a small heavy object hitting the stone floor.

"What the fuck was that?" Cock whispered.

"Judging by the feel of the slightly warm liquid congealing on my fingers I'd say that it was the sound of Duke dying," Pock replied.

"What! Who killed him?"

"How the fuck should I know? I can't see a fucking thing."

Pock muttered something under his breath, and a small yellow ball appeared in the air. It slowly floated up to the ceiling where it attached itself.

The two brothers looked across at the chair where that Duke had been sat. The Duke's body was still there, but his head was lay sideways on the floor a look of surprise on it. There was a pool of blood around the head, but strangely there was no blood fountaining out of the stump at the top of the body.

"Well, that is fucking weird and no mistake." Said Pock

The buzzing began to get louder again, and Pock just had enough time to put a magical shield up to deflect whatever was coming towards himself and his brother.

It was a six-inch wide disk that was no more than two millimetres thick and with razor sharp edges. As it flew in towards Pock, it bounced off the shield and flew straight up and embedded itself into the wooden ceiling.

Pock and Cock watched fascinated as the blade vibrated back and forth trying to pull itself free of the wood.

"What the fuck is that?" Whispered Cock.

Tales from Ashen Falls

"Beats me because I haven't seen anything like that before.'

The buzzing was becoming more and more high pitched and frantic as the disk wobbled backwards and forwards.

"We need to do something to nullify that before it gets loose, and we both end up a head shorter. Like Duke." Pock nodded towards Duke's body.

A voice came from around the corner of the inn, beyond the radius of the small light that Pock had conjured earlier. It was too far away for the two brothers to make out any of the words. It sounded like the voice was muffled, perhaps coming from behind a door.

A second voice shushed the first and sounded clearer.

Pock looked over at Cock and shrugged his shoulders. From behind his back, he retrieved a dagger. The weapon's blade was so long that it was practically a short sword. One side of the blade was serrated while the other side gave off a soft blue light. The whole blade was pitted as if it had pock marks all over it too.

Meanwhile, Cock had produced a huge crossbow. The crossbow had a huge bear bolt sitting ready to fire; its huge four-bladed tips seemed to gleam with a malevolence all of its own.

Pock gestured with his head for his brother to go to the left of the room, then he pointed to himself and nodded to the right.

As Pock made his way around several tables, he kept hearing grunting and incomprehensible talking. He hoped to all the Gods that he wasn't about to find two people having sex.

However, as he advanced the words began to become clearer.

"I can't open the bloody thing!'
"Hnk Graa Knaaf."
"What? I don't know what you're saying, wait a moment and I'll try my dagger."
"Negs whet ay seed."
"Really? That's nice."

There was the sound of a dagger being thrust into something wooden.

"Ble clarbful."
"Ha! I understood that, don't worry I'll be careful."
"Whad abowd de bownters band de mamader?"

"Oh don't worry about those three. I ensorceled the Spinner to kill three targets, and it won't stop until it has killed them."

"Sbunner?"

"Just a little something I invented to help in my line of work. It doesn't do to get caught digging up bodies you know."

Pock had had time to position himself as close as he could without alerting the two voices to his presence. He had managed to work out that the two voices were male, but he didn't recognise either of them.

He didn't have a clue what was going on behind the bar counter, but one of the men sounded like he had a really heavy cold.

What he did know was that this wasn't a robbery. There had been no attempt to open the till behind the bar and all the bottles of liquor still stood in their usual places.

Pock looked over to where his brother crouched against the other end of the bar and even as he looked his brother disappeared. He smiled then uttered a word, and he too vanished.

Slowly the brothers stood up and looked over the bar.

Tales from Ashen Falls

Hunkered down on the floor was the ginger-haired man from that morning, a dagger in his hand. In front of him was the box that contained The Dove's head.

"Cumb om." The head spoke to the man in front of him.

"I'm trying my best! I'm a bloody necromancer, not a thief, and if you don't stop nagging, I'll cancel the spell that brought you back to life."

"I bare do."

"If it wasn't for the loot, you know the location of I would, but I want that loot. You have no idea how our family have suffered since you got caught all those years ago. We even had to leave Ashen Falls great grandad."

The head inside the case frowned, "Whag loog?"

The man stopped trying to pry the case open, "Whag...What loot he says. The loot you had on you when you were caught."

The man seemed to realise what he had just said, and his face began to turn purple, "Aw, shit!"

The head in the case began to laugh which wasn't a pretty sight for anyone to see.

The man face was bright beetroot as he stood up, "Stop laughing or by the Gods I'll break this case and stomp on your bloody head!"

The disembodied head kept laughing, and the man raised his right leg and brought it down towards the case. Spittle flecked from his open mouth, and his face was twisted with hate.

Things began to happen fast as shards of glass and splinters of wood went flying all over the bar floor. The fluid that head had been sitting in splashed across the bottles, bar and ground.

The crossbow in Cocks hand gave a sudden lurch as the huge bolt shot out of its cradle. The black point of the bolt flew straight into the man's open mouth with such force that it ripped the man's head clean off the spinal column. The bolt then carried the head through the air before pinning the head to the wall behind.

Now that The Dove's head was free of the case he let out a scream of despair, "Nooo!"

Pock watched as the man's body fell to the ground, blood spurting from torn flesh and making an even bigger mess behind the bar.

Tales from Ashen Falls

Those bottles will all need a good clean, he thought.

Cock jumped over the bar top and landed without a sound on the other side.

Pock did the same next to where he stood.

Moving cautiously forward so that they didn't slip and fall over the two brothers looked at the carnage around them.

"You fucking idiots, what did you do that for?"

The brothers looked down at The Dove's head.

"Are you talking to us?" Replied Pock indignantly.

"Well, I don't see any other fucking idiots around here! The first chance in I don't know how fucking long to get out of this fucking box and you kill the imbecile before he could find me a body!"

Pock sneered at the head, "For someone without a body you certainly do walk the walk."

"Fuck you!"

"That's going to be very difficult in your condition."

Tales from Ashen Falls

Cock walked around the mess as best he could and proceeded over to the wall from which the head was impaled.

Reaching up he took hold of the bear bolt and just as quickly pulled his hand back when the head blinked. The ginger haired head tried to talk, but the quarrel was filling too much of his mouth.

Anyway, Cock wasn't interested in what it had to say, raising the crossbow he began to smack the stock into the head until the skull shattered and brains exploded in all directions.

"Fucking necromancers. I fucking hate necromancers. Every time they cast a spell you get the smell of rotting flesh."

Pock nodded at The Dove, "It's true he does hate them."

The Dove cleared his throat, "That's nice but I could do with a little help here."

"No offence friend but we need to get a new case to put you in."

"No! Please don't, I just want to be free. To be a man again, to live and love. Please help me, I'll be no trouble, promise."

Pock lowered himself closer to The Dove, "Well, there is something you could do..."

Tales from Ashen Falls

"Just name it, please!"

"Inn needs a new manager."

"I'll do it. All I need is a body with plenty of blood still in it."

"Well, then this one's no good then." Said Pock nudging the ginger haired man's corpse with his foot, "Hang on, though. I have an idea. You can have Duke's old body; all we have to do is get it. Wait here."

"Where the fuck am I supposed to go?"

Pock jumped back over the bar and made his way towards the table at the back. Taking a quick look at the ceiling, he noticed a deep gouge in the wood, but the disk was gone. Looking at the floor, he could see no sign of it there either.

He gripped the handle of his dagger tighter, the knuckles on his hand turning white with the pressure. With a quick word, he renewed the light spell that he had used earlier. Then with another word he created a perfect image of himself.

Beads of sweat had started to appear on his forehead as he exerted his magic. Here and there the hairs on his head started to turn grey.

Tales from Ashen Falls

With a flick of his wrist, the duplicate began to move towards the area of the table.

There was a sudden buzzing as the disk suddenly appeared and flew at the apparition. If the image had been the real Pock, he would have been decapitated. The disk flew on a bit more before spinning back towards the illusion.

Pock began to manoeuvre the image so that the disk would hit one of the walls. If he could get the disk stuck, he could hopefully neutralise the disk.

The spinning blade came to a stop and began to circle the illusion. If Pock didn't know any better, he would have thought it was sniffing the air.

Suddenly it was flying through the air as Cock ran into the room. The spinning disk bit into his neck and he fell to the ground wordlessly. Blood sprayed in fine droplets from the deep gash where the blade had stuck.

"Bastard!" Pock screamed and ran towards his dying brother. Tears streamed down his face as he kneeled down.

The disk buzzed as it tried in vain to get loose from Cocks neck.

Tales from Ashen Falls

Full of anger Pock touched the disk and sent a blast of electricity into the weapon. Sparks flew from the disks centre and with a loud bang all life left the disk.

Pock cradled his brother's head and wept, his tears falling on his brother's face.

He didn't look up as footsteps approached, didn't wonder who it might be. His world had been torn away from under him. How was he supposed to go on living without his brother? What was he going to tell the chickens?

"What the fuck is wrong with you?"

"My brothers dead and you're wondering what's wrong. Fucking insensitive…"

Cock removed the illusion he had put on the hat stand upon which he had cast an animation spell.

"I will be dead soon if I keep those spells going." He smiled at his brother.

Pock placed the end of the hat stand down, "You bastard! You absolute fucking bastard!"

"Is it my fault that I'm better at illusions and animation than you?"

Then the two brothers were hugging and laughing. At one point Pock even thought about doing a little jig but wisely changed his mind.

"Come on, give me a hand with this body and head," Pock said.

The two brothers retrieved the parts formally known as Duke and took them into the bar area. Even though Cock was starting to look a little older than Pock, he had been given the task of putting the case back together using magic.

"What are we going to do to keep it fresh?"

Pock located a couple of bottles of Alvarian potato wine and handed them to his brother, "Here, use these."

As Cock filled the case up with the wine, Pock looked down at The Dove's head, "Any idea how this is going to work?"

"Just put my neck to the body's neck and we should bind together."

"Hmm, I'm not sure that's going to work because his necks been cauterised."

"Oh."

"I know! I'll just slice a bit off."

"Aye, that should be alright."

Taking his dagger, Pock sliced through the flesh with ease. Blood started to seep out of the fresh cut neck. Taking The Dove's head, he placed the two ends of the neck together.

A few seconds later the head began to look more alive. Colour began to return to the skin, and the eyes seemed to gleam again.

Even though it was a bit late in the day, Pock looked just to make sure that the head and body were facing the same way. It would be embarrassing if the man could watch himself taking a shit.

He let out a sigh of relief when he saw that the two parts were fine.

Soon The Dove was able to sit up, and Duke's head was safely ensconced in the display case.

Pock looked at Cock and wiped his hands on a cloth, "Time to go home."

Cock nodded, "Aye, I'm knackered."

The Dove called after the two brothers, "Wait! What about me?"

Pock turned, "Well you've got a body to dispose of, a load of blood, brains and skull fragments to clear up, bottles to wash clean and then and only then do you get to go to bed. Good night."

Tales from Ashen Falls

With that, the two brothers left The Dove's Head Inn and started heading home to their hovel.

"Think I should have stayed in the box." The Dove muttered to himself as he went off to find the stuff he would need to clean up.

Tales from Ashen Falls

Tales from Ashen Falls

Melress Investigates

Melress had enjoyed a day off from his training as a Battle Mage and was making his way back to the fortress that stood sentinel over the city of Ashen Falls.

Even though he was off duty, he still had to be back before curfew as he was still a minor. At thirteen years old he had been a trainee battle mage for six years.

He was glad he wasn't one of the Mages that had to learn all the different types of flora that could be used to cast spells. That with a simple word or two he could call forth fire, water, wind even lightning. In fact, anything he wanted to really and as a half-elf he could keep his spells going for quite a long time.

Half-elves lived hundreds of years and casting spells caused the user to age quicker. In some extreme cases, the person can become consumed by the power, and it was not unheard of for a mage to die of old age from power drain.

Melress's Battle Mage training had consisted of learning to wear and repair armour, use and fix weapons and learning techniques including how to keep himself calm so that he didn't succumb to the power.

To be fair, he quite liked being a battle mage; he only had one problem, and that was a fellow student by the name of Ellowe. Ellowe was a human, and he had made Melress's life a misery on and off since Melress had joined.

Melress would usually get two weeks off at a time, and he would visit his friend Princess Beatrice of Hamerband, but sometimes if he were just given a day or two, he would stay in Ashen Falls and use the local facilities.

Melress turned into an alley hoping to make up time and came to an abrupt halt.

There was a body lying face down about ten feet into the alley. A dark puddle covered the area around the person's head like a corona.

Melress cast a small spell that deflected the smell of blood and allowed clean, fresh air through.

A raven flapped down to land beside the body and cocked its head to one side. It regarded the corpse with its beady black eyes. Having taken in the scene before it, the Raven spoke, "He's dead."

Tales from Ashen Falls

"Thanks for clearing that up for me Caw, anything else you care to enlighten me with?"

"Looks like his throat has been ripped out by some wild animal. Judging by the congealing blood, the body has been here a while. Long enough for it to have been spotted and reported, I would have thought."

Melress sighed and moved closer to the body, his spell allowing him to breathe easily.

Normal thirteen-year-olds would have run screaming and sobbing, but Melress had experienced several adventures in his life already.

He walked around the body and noted that it was a man and that he was wearing expensive clothing. Several gold rings were on the man's fingers, and a gold earring was visible through his ear.

"Not a robbery then," Melress said to Caw

Caw didn't reply. Instead, he took wing as the sound of footsteps and armour jangling could be heard approaching.

"Well, well. What do we have here?"

The speaker was a male elf; he was wearing chain mail over which was a tabard depicting the sign of the city watch on it – a circle that was half red and half black to depict the top of a volcano when active and dormant. At his right hip was a sheathed long sword and from this Melress deduced that the man was left-handed.

Great, why did have to be an elf? Thought Melress

As a half-elf, many elves looked upon Melress as some freak, an abomination in the eyes of the Elven Gods – The Seven. Melress was alright in the Battle Mages as they were from all three races. Melress considered himself fortunate that elves tended just to make life difficult for him rather than commit acts of outright violence. Of course, the purple badge pinned to his chest probably helped with that as anyone who saw it knew Melress was a Battle Mage.

"Nothing to say, murderer?"

Melress cleared his throat, "I didn't kill him."

"That's what they all say, although most add guv on the end for some reason."

The watchman's eyes narrowed as he looked the young Half-Elf up and down.

Here we go, thought Melress

"Battle Mage, eh?"

Tales from Ashen Falls

"Yes, Sir. Trainee actually and I swear I didn't kill him. I've only just got here myself."

The mans eyes were drawn to Caw as the bird returned to land on Melress's shoulder.

"Fu...Blimey that's a big crow lad!"

"He's a raven, Sir, but yes he is big. Weighs a bit even with hollow bones."

Melress thought that the man was smiling judging by the crinkles he could see appear around the eyes.

"Half-Elf as well, eh?"

"Is that a problem, Sir?"

"Lad, it makes no difference to me. I've seen the bad side of all of the races and all the good side too...Not as often, though. The only thing that interests me is catching the thing that killed Gold Thom."

"Old Thom?"

"No lad, Gold Thom. I knew it was him as soon all those gold rings on that hand. He's a money lender out of The Vile."

The Vile was the most deprived are of Ashen Falls and was where most of the thieves and malcontents lived. No one with any sense went there covered in gold, the question that sprang to mind was what was he doing here?

Tales from Ashen Falls

The watchman saw the look on Melress's face, "Oh, he didn't live there. He lived in Merchant's Row, had a suite of rooms over one of the shops. He must have been coming or going from The Vile."

"Well, like I said I didn't kill him."

"I know lad. If you had, there wouldn't be a body, and I wouldn't still be standing here. The question is who did? The list is probably as long as the occupants of this city."

"Well, Sir perhaps I can be of some help. All I ask is that you tell my Captain that I was helping you out so that I don't get into trouble."

"It's a deal, lad. You can call me Asperal."

Melress nodded, "Melress."

"So how are you going to help me, Melress?"

"I'll need a bit more time examining the scene, but I reckon he's been here a while."

"I agree. He's starting to smell a bit, and that's always a good sign of how long a body has been lying."

"One thing concerns me."

"What's that?"

"Apart from the throat, the body has no other wounds which means that the local dogs, cats and even rats haven't worried the corpse."

"Hmm. I will admit that is a bit odd, but what does it tell us?"

"To be honest, at the moment I'm using magic to filter fresh air into my nose so I can't smell anything at all."

Caw spoke to Melress, which came out as load of cawing, to Asperal, "I can, a sharp, tangy smell."

Melress looked at Asperal, "Do you know anything that leaves a sharp, tangy smell behind it?"

"Hmm, it reminds me of something, but I don't remember what exactly. I'll have a think, and I'm sure it will come to me, though."

"If you remember I might be able to track the murderer."

"Don't rush me Melress. I think it stems back to my time as scout. It was a while ago, and my old brain isn't what it used to be."

Melress took a deep breath and hunkered down next to the body and looked at the ragged wound. There were four marks beginning at the side of the throat. The marks got deeper as they came around the front of the neck. In the gaping hole, Melress could see glistening tubes and flesh.

He watched as a fly started to approach the wound, it seemed to do a double take and fly off in the other direction.

"Even the flies don't seem to like him."

Asperal looked at the Battle Mage, "What did you say?"

"I said, even the flies aren't going near the body."

"That's it."

"What's it?"

"That smell is Yaruk urine. That's what's keeping everything away, but it must be almost gone so I wouldn't be surprised if it stops keeping the animals off in an hour or so."

Melress thought back to his lessons. The Yaruk was a big cat that lived in heavily forested, mountainous regions. Commonly found between the Borderlands and the Orc Lands the cats were three feet long from head to tip of the tail. They also had large paw pads that distributed the weight of the cat, and this made them very hard to track.

Tales from Ashen Falls

If this was a Yaruk attack how had the cat managed to get into Ashen Falls?

There was a scream from several streets over. Melress cast a spell, and a faint blue line appeared on the ground.

While Melress cast his spell, Caw took to the air, his large, powerful wings beating him into the sky.

Both Melress and Asperal had raised their heads in an attempt to determine the direction of the scream.

Melress looked at the blue line on the ground, "I guess we just need to follow that!"

"What is it?"

"I cast a location spell for a big cat based on the direction of the scream. This line should take us there… or as near as possible anyway."

Asperal drew his longsword from its sheath and started to follow the line with Melress following behind."

The blue line took them down three streets and across four alleys to eventually come out on Main Street. Down the street, the two of them could see The Dove's Head Inn. Two lanterns were lit on either side of the door but at this time of night there were no bouncers stood outside.

Tales from Ashen Falls

Almost in the middle of the street lay the body of a woman, a pool of blood was fanning out from her torn throat and her golden eyes stared sightlessly at the approaching figures.

As they approached, they recoiled, not from the body but the smell of Yaruk urine. Melress improved the breathing spell, and the smell disappeared. Asperal had no such luxury and had to pinch his nose with his free hand.

From The Dove's Head Inn came a clatter as the door was thrown open and two men stepped out. They were identically dressed in black shirts and trousers. One of the men had a face covered in pock marks, and both men had black eyes.

The one with the pock marks was holding the longest knife Melress had ever seen while the other man had a crossbow with a bear bolt loaded ready to fire.

Asperal moved to stand next to Melress his longsword held ready to bring up if necessary.

The pockmarked man spoke first, "Asperal. What's going on? Is that Yaruk piss I can smell?"

The other man looked alarmed at the mention of the Yaruk and sniffed the air. His face crinkled in distaste, "Better keep away from my fucking chickens, that's all I can say!"

Melress wondered how the first man had recognised Asperal when the man wore a helmet. He also expected Asperal to tell them to mind their own business but instead pointed down at the body.

"Got a dead woman here and I've got a dead Gold Thom seven streets over."

The man holding the blade laughed, "Thom's dead?"

"Aye."

"They'll be weeping in the streets in the morning."

Melress was confused, he thought the man was unpopular.

"Aye, many's the people who will be weeping tears of joy at that bastard's death, Pock."

Pock nodded in agreement before turning his attention to the body in front of them, "Who is it?"

"Don't know."

Pock leant down to have a closer look, "Looks like one of the girls who work out of The Vile."

Asperal looked at Pock, "A Whore then?"

Cock's finger tensed on the crossbow as Pock answered, "Not all the people in The Vile are bad Asperal, some have jobs same as my brother and me. She was a waitress at one of those fancy restaurants the rich folk go to."

Asperal's mouth pursed as Pock carried on talking, "Gold Thom worked The Vile didn't he? Seems like a connection to me."

"Aye, looks like I'm off into The Vile."
"Alone?"
"I've got Melress here."

He nodded towards Melress as he spoke.

"A boy? I don't think he's going to be much back up. D'you want me and Cock to come with you."

"He's a Battle Mage."
"I'm a Battle Mage."

Pock smiled again, "Couse you are, son!"

Tales from Ashen Falls

Melress pulled his shirt forward so that the two men could see his badge.

"Oh well, in that case, you two should be fine then."

Asperal motioned towards the Inn, "You two gentlemen may as well get back inside. We'll deal with this."

Pock looked as if he was about to say something then turned to his brother, "Come on."

No sooner had the men closed the Inn door than Melress and Asperal heard a roar from one of the side alleys.

Rushing towards the sound the pair of them saw a large cat moving down the middle of the alley heading further in The Vile.

High above Caw circled over the cat so that it could be tracked more easily. He didn't see that Asperal had moved slightly behind Melress.

When the two figures were far enough into the alley, Asperal called out, "Ayusha!"

The cat stopped and turned at the sound of her name. Melress tensed and then he felt cold steel press into his back.

"Ayusha, my pet, come to daddy."

Tales from Ashen Falls

Melress sighed, what an idiot he had been. The man who had brought the cat into the city had been right beside him the whole time.

"The Yaruk is yours?"

"Yes, I'm afraid so Melress."

"And you're training it to kill people?"

"Only people from The Vile. It's my experience that scum like them have a certain odour, crime seems to ooze out of every pore that they possess."

Ayusha padded closer to Melress and Asperal. It sniffed the air, and both of them could see it's fangs gleam in the moonlight.

There would be nothing Melress could do when the cat leapt at him, not with Asperal's sword at his back. He was dead either way and wondered why he wasn't already.

"But why?"

"Why? Why do you think? Every day I have to work in this shit hole, to see the worst excesses of the depraved that call it home. Half the time when I arrest anyone they're back out in an hour. So killing them seemed like a good idea. I have contacts from when I was a scout, and I've raised cats before, so I thought why not?"

"What about me?"

"What about you? We will retrace our steps, and you will burn the bodies to remove any trace and then I will kill you, a rogue Battle Mage."

Suddenly the big cat tensed and leapt towards Melress, and all he could do was close his eyes and pray to whatever God Half-Elves had.

There was a scream followed by a thump, a thud followed by a screech. Melress stood for a few seconds and then tentatively opened one eye.

Well, I'm still alive at least, he thought.

He looked down at the ground, and there lay Asperal with his throat neatly torn out. Beside him lay Ayusha with a long dagger sticking from her ribs, but she was still breathing. Fast, shallow breaths came from her as she fought for life.

Out of the shadows strode the two men from The Dove's Head Inn.

Pock nodded at Melress, "Never did trust that man."

He looked over at his companion, "Cock, finish the cat off if you would be so kind."

Tales from Ashen Falls

Melress started, "No!"

"You can't be serious lad; it's killed three people. It has to die."

Melress knew that the man was right. Even though Ayusha was a beautiful animal, she had killed and would likely kill again.

As cock moved closer to the animal, the cat give a shuddering breath and died.

Pock looked at Melress, "We need to move these bodies. Do you think you can bring the cat?"

"Yes, Sir."

"Names Pock, lad, and that ugly fucker over there is my brother, Cock."

Melress nodded and began to put magic into his arms, making them stronger. This wasn't his Mage magic but his other magic because Mages couldn't cast spells that directly affected people.

With hardly any effort at all, he picked up the large cat and followed the two brothers.

Later they all stood in a line watching as the fire that poured from Pock's fingers cremated the four bodies.

Soon all that was left were four scorch marks on the cobble which Cock then removed with magic of his own.

Melress stared at the two men in disbelief, "You two are Battle Mages?"

"We used to be, lad, we used to be."

Pock picked up a small bag which contained all the coins and jewellery from the victims.

"We'll see that this little lot goes to them that need it most."

In his other hand was a sealed note, "Give this to your Captain when you get back, you should be okay."

Melress took the note, "Thanks."

Then he turned and started back to the fortress.

Once Melress had left the two brothers alone, Cock walked up to his brother, "Is he the one?"

Pock smiled, "Aye. Dark days are coming brother, but I think we have a few years yet."

Tales from Ashen Falls

Tales from Ashen Falls

The Scarecrow

Every night when The Dove's Head Inn closed, the two bouncers that have stood outside would head indoors and play a hand or three of cards with the eponymous Dove.

In The Dove's Head Inn this was called team building.

Unusually for the time of year, a thick fog curled its way around the city streets. Here and there groups of city watchmen went about their business, but they had little chance of catching criminals with the lack of visibility.

In the richer parts of Ashen Falls, many of the buildings were clear, their owners employing a Mage to deflect the fog from their properties. Unfortunately, this caused the fog to thicken the further you travelled from the posh quarter.

Down in The Vile, a young boy of eight years was searching through the detritus around one of the sewer exits.

Fug came here once or twice a week in the hope that something valuable would have flushed out of the sewer. As he approached nearer to the outlet he could smell rotting flesh and the closer he got the worse it got.

Fug rubbed his hands together; a body could be a good find – if it still had something on it that could be sold. He wasn't too worried about the fact the corpse stunk worse than one of his nan's farts. He had been scavenging on the streets for as long as he could remember.

He had been doing it ever since his mother had stabbed his father when she came home early and found him in bed with another woman.

To be fair it wasn't that that had caused his wife to pick up the only decent knife they had, it was the fact that his father had locked nan out in the outside privy while he had sex.

Nan and his mother had disposed of the corpse in the dead of night. Fug didn't ask where, but he took it upon himself to start earning a wage to help out. Knowing that his mother wouldn't want him thieving, he had turned to scavenging. If he was lucky, he made as much as a silver shiny a month.

Fug moved a piece of wooden board, and the smell from underneath nearly made him gag. Taking a dirty scarf from around his neck, he wrapped it over his mouth and nose.

The corpse seemed to be missing a head. It was wearing black trousers and boots; the torso was covered in an off white silk shirt with yellow thread.

That should be worth a copper head, he thought, *of course; it will all need a clean.*

Fug started to take the clothes off the body; he noticed that the skin was white, and the stomach was bloated. He slowed down and became more careful as the stomach could explode from all the gas trapped inside it and if he breathed that in he could expect a long, lingering death.

Even working slowly, he soon had all the clothing off the body, and he began to make his way home.

The fog seemed even thicker as he wended his way around the streets back to where he lived with his mother and nan. He was nearly home when a hand grabbed his shoulder making him jump.

"What ya got there, Fug?"

Fug sighed, he knew things had been going too well, "Just some rags, Shard; that's all. Nothing you'd be interested in."

Tales from Ashen Falls

Shard was five years older than Fug and had lived on the streets of The Vile for as long as he could remember. He had gotten his name from the sharp piece of glass he had slot into a length of wood. Rumour had it that he wasn't afraid to use his shiv for the slightest of reasons."

"I'll be the judge of that. Lie it all down on the ground and let's take a look."

Fug didn't dare argue with the older boy; he didn't want to get cut, and the clothes certainly weren't worth being killed over. Slowly he placed the items on the cold, uneven cobbles.

Shard looked unimpressed, "What a load of shit!"

Then he leant forward and scrutinised the shirt and boots. They looked as if they might fit him, "I'll 'av the shirt and boots, Fug, you can keep the rest of the shit."

Fug picked up the trousers. Tears were beginning to form in the corner of his eyes, and he didn't want Shard to see. Scrunching the trousers into a ball he continued on his way home. At least he could say that he was still alive!

Shard put the shirt on first then waited until the younger boy had left the street before sitting down to try the boots on proper. He took off the battered shoes he had been wearing, which were more holes than leather and flung them to the other side of the street. A rat squealed as one of the shoes bounced into it; it looked over at Shard with baleful eyes before scampering away.

    Shard pulled one of the boots on. At first, he thought it was too big for his foot and then after wriggling his toes it seemed to be a perfect fit. He put it down to the suppleness of the leather and put the other boot on.

    This turned out to be Shards biggest and last mistake. Green fog began to pour from Shards mouth as he tried desperately to scream. Little flashes of green lightening ran across his eyes before exploding and rendering the boy blind. He flailed about the deserted, foggy street before collapsing on the ground.

    Time passed, one minute then two and suddenly the body twitched and began to rise from the ground. From empty eye sockets, green fire danced and whirled.

    "Oh no, this won't do at all!"

    The voice that came from Shards mouth sounded much older. It muttered indistinguishable words and suddenly arched it's back as bones began to grow and thrust out of the flesh that housed them. Soon the figure resembled a human porcupine, and once the transformation was complete, it began to head out of The Vile towards The Dove's Head Inn.

This time, he would emerge the victor against those two idiot bouncers and his great grandfather.

Meanwhile, Pock, Cock and Dove were just having their fourth round of cards. The two brothers were in no hurry to head home in the fog, and the ale was going down nicely.

Dove jumped as a scream sounded from outside the Inn, "What the fuck was that?"

Pock brought his hands up to his head and touched his temples with the index fingers, "Hold on, I'll just use my psychic abilities."

Dove looked suitably impressed, "I never knew you had psychic abilities."

Cock shook his head and started laughing.

Pock sighed, "I don't, it was sarcasm."

"Oh right. Well, that's nice and all but we still don't know what made that scream."

"And what would we do if we did. My advice is not to get involved unless trouble comes knocking."

There were several bangs on the door to the Inn.

"I couldn't write this shit if I tried."

Suddenly Pock had his long dagger in his hand, and Cock had his crossbow ready. Dove looked put out, "I would love to know how you two do that."

Dove emptied his mag of ale and prepared to use it as a club.

Pock shook his head in amazement, "That is going to go down as the worst weapon in history."

"Fuck off; it's all that's to hand. I'll be pissed if I neck the jug down."

More knocking sound came from the door, and the three men spread out and approached it.

Pock reached out to turn the key that stuck out from the door while Cock stood off to one side the crossbow held firm and steady. Dove moved to the side of the door and raised his mug above his head.

Tales from Ashen Falls

The key turned smoothly in its lock and apart from the continued banging nothing happened.

Pock reached out with a steady hand and turned the handle. A figure came hurtling into the Inn. At first, the three men thought it was a large man flailing his arms and legs in all directions until they realised that it was one man with two small children hanging off him.

The two children were chewing into the man's flesh and blood was dripping out of a dozen or more bites already.

The man screamed more in anger than in pain as the two children tried to bite through his scalp.

Cock looked at Pock, "What do we do? We can't kill kids!"

As he spoke, one of the children stopped trying to chew on the man on the ground and whirled towards this new source of food.

Pock took a quick look outside and up the street. At the periphery of his vision, he could see more children lumbering towards them.

Tales from Ashen Falls

He slammed the door shut and locked it before turning his attention back to the inside of the Inn.

The man was lay on the floor holding his head and groaning, the boy who had been trying to eat him was lay flat out, while Dove stood looking at the handle of his mug even as the rest of it rolled on the floor in a lazy circle.

Pock was using the cocking stirrup to keep the child at bay, but he couldn't do it forever.

Pock flipped his dagger over and brought the pommel crashing down on the child's head. The child fell to the floor unconscious.

The man had stopped moaning and started to get up. The man's mouth opened, and he give a groan then lurched towards Pock.

Cock raised the crossbow and pressed the trigger. The bolt took most of the man's face off, and he fell back to the floor.

Dove looked about him for another weapon, "I suppose I'll have to clean that fucking mess up before I can go to bed!" He complained.

He picked up one of the chairs as he was speaking.

"Don't break too many of those or the customers will have nothing to sit on." Cock observed.

The two children were starting to stir again, moans and groans escaping from their lips.

Pock knocked them both unconscious again, but they couldn't keep doing that all night and...

There was suddenly more banging coming from the front of the Inn, not just from the door this time but from the whole of the front.

Dove placed the chair back down and went off to the store room where he knew that there was some rope. They would have to tie the two kids up until they could get them to a Priest. They had probably eaten something that hadn't agreed with them.

Outside the inn and stood behind the dozen or so street children that he had managed to capture and kill stood what used to be the ginger haired man.

He had decided to call himself The Scarecrow on account of the fact that they scared birds, and he was going to scare a certain Dove to his grave.

It was a bit of a bastard that the three men had managed to lock the door before his little army could get inside, but he was a Necromancer after all. All he needed to do was think of a plan.

From behind him came the sound of marching boots and a lantern cut its way through the fog.

The children at the Inn turned as a voice yelled, "Oi! What do you lot think you're up to?"

The Scarecrow smiled as the children descended on the three city watchmen and started to bite on any exposed flesh. It wouldn't take long before the three men were infected and then he would have some swords on his side.

Inside The Dove's Head Inn, the three men looked at each other as the sounds of screams rose into the air.

Cock spoke first, "Hopefully, that will bring the watch running."

Tales from Ashen Falls

Pock shook his head, "It depends what happens to the watch once they get here."

Dove started to sniff, "Has one of you farted?"

Pock and Cock took a deep sniff.

Pocks face crinkled up, "That's the smell of rot and given the state of those two children I would say we have another Necromancer problem."

There came the sound of metal hitting the door, and Cock made his way to the window to take a look. Outside he could see a dozen frenzied children and three members of the city watch trying to break the door down with swords.

Behind the crowd of crazy bastards was a...a thing. It had green fire for eyes and bone sticking out from its body. Cock recognised what was left of the figures shirt and turned to Dove.

"Dove, what did you do with the remains of your Necromantic relative?"

Dove looked abashed, "Why?"

He started to move to the window with Pock following closely behind. The two men looked outside with Cock; they had loads of time; swords were rubbish for chopping down doors.

    Cock looked at Dove, "Recognise anything about the one at the back, like say, the shirt?"

    "Oh."

    Pock put his hand up to his nose and pinched it, "That explains why I saw them all heading for the Inn. I guess that fellow on the floor just got unlucky."

    Cock raised his crossbow and looked as if he was going to fire it through the window, "I don't know if I've mentioned this before but I fucking hate Necromancers."

    Pock put a hand on his brother's shoulder, "I know you do, but we have to keep focused. Clearly, someone in this room did a sloppy job of clearing up."

    "Hey, I cleaned up. The body must have come out of the sewer nearby."

    Both brothers spoke together, "You dumped him in the sewer?"

    Pock shook his head, "You use fire, you idiot. Make sure nothing survives because you can be sure that they will have something magical on them to bring 'em back."

"Well I didn't know that, but I do now."

"Bit fucking late don't ya think?"

"Sorry lads, so what do we do now?"

"I hate to say it but were going to have to kill everyone out there and those two kids in here too."

"We can't just kill the children out of hand." Dove decided he was going to hold the moral high ground on this one, "You said so yourself."

Pock's face was haggard and drawn at the enormity of the decision he had to make, "Dove, they aren't children anymore. They've been killed and brought back from the dead to kill us."

"But what about their families?"

"By the looks of 'em, they either don't have any or their families don't care. I don't like this anymore than you Dove, but it's gotta be done."

"Like history repeating." Muttered Cock

"What's that Cock?"

Cock looked at Dove with moist eyes, "Have I ever told you I fucking really, really hate Necromancers?"

"Once or twice, but you haven't said why."

Cock looked at dove for a couple of heartbeats breathing heavily through his nose, "No…"

Dove stood there with a look that seemed to say, *Well…*

Pock spoke into the silence the two men had created, "Drop it, Dove. We need to do something before our ginger haired friend can find someone with an axe."

Cock seemed to come out of a trance, "What's the plan, brother?"

"Well there's no need for subtlety, Dove can fling the door open and as they rush in we can deal with them. Oh, and this time we finish the job off on the Necromancer."

"Simple but effective, hopefully."

Dove looked from brother to brother, "Hang on, how exactly are you going to deal with them?"

The two brothers muttered a word and flames danced around their hands. Dove looked pissed, "Oh, that's just great that is. Two bloody Battle Mages and you never thought to say anything before? Thought we were mates."

Tales from Ashen Falls

Cock looked at Pock who nodded imperceptibly.

"Here's a little secret for you Dove, we ain't Battle Mages."

"Well, what kind of mages are you?"

"Too be honest were not Mages at all."

Dove pointed to the flames leaping and dancing from the brother's hands, "Ahem, which would prove you to be really bad liars."

Pock smiled, "We're not lying, Dove, we really aren't Mages."

"So what are you then?"

Pock smile widened, "We're Gods of course! Now open the door and let's save ourselves because there ain't no-one else around to do it."

Dove opened the door while muttering about *'piss taking bastards'*.

Pock and Cock smiled and shook their heads behind Doves back.

Then they were shooting bolts of flame out through the open door as the dead children and just as dead city watchmen tried to force themselves through the doorway.

They burned without a sound as the flames leapt from the brother's hands to melt the flesh of the foes before them. The brother's hair started to turn grey and wrinkles started to appear.

Dove watched as the flames killed again and again and the two men got older and older, "Gods my arse. Gods wouldn't age that quickly. I knew they were trying to trick me."

One of the undead children had managed to sneak past the two Battle Mages and ran at Dove. As he neared, Dove brought the chair down on the child's head. The chair smashed into pieces as it hit leaving Dove holding one leg. He raised the led and brought it crashing down again and again. Blood, brains and skull fragments went flying in all directions.

Looking down at what was left of the child, Dove muttered, "I fucking hate Necromancers."

The Scarecrow looked on as his small army was burnt to a crisp, "Bastards! Now what to do?"

The problem with being a Necromancer was that it didn't lend itself to off the cuff magic. No fireballs or lightning bolts for him.

Then again the two Battle Mages were almost spent and his great grandfather was no fighter, whereas he had wielded knives ever since his first dissection at eight years old. He reached into his waistband and pulled out the shard of glass that was kept there. At one end it had been attached to a piece of stick that had been wrapped in rags to keep the two pieces firm.

    Not exactly the blade of choice for the dapper Necromancer about town, but it will do the job just nicely.

    The three men before him stepped over the piles of ashes that lay all around them and fanned out into a semi-circle.

    The two bouncers were puffing and panting as they stood looking at the baleful presence before them.

    Yes! They were both spent up.

    "What's the matter with you two? Look at you; you look like you're one hundred. Not looking quite so tough now are you?"

    The two brothers pointed at the figure standing before them and chains flew from their fingers to ensnare The Scarecrow. The Scarecrow decided that now was as good a time as any to start begging for mercy, "Please don't hurt me!"

Pock huffed, "It's... not... us... you... have... to... worry... about..."

"Oh no? So who should I worry about?"

Pock gestured vaguely behind The Scarecrow, "Them."

"That's the oldest trick in the book; you really think I'm going to fall for that one."

Strong hands clamped down on each of The Scarecrows shoulders and lifted him off the ground. The Scarecrow struggled to free himself from the steely grip that held him, but to no avail.

He found himself being turned around and carried off through the streets of Ashen Falls.

Dove dropped the bloodied chair leg to the ground, then started jumping around as one of the nails in the end stuck into his foot.

Eventually, he stopped hopping about and looked at the two brothers, "What exactly did I just witness?"

Tales from Ashen Falls

Pock shook his head, "I don't think you're quite ready to know the truth. Let's just say the Brotherhood of Battle Mages came and took the Necromancer away."

"Fuck that; I want the truth."

Pock sighed, "The two men who took that piece of shit away were called Law and Childhood, and it seems that they took exception to the Necromancers actions."

"What will they do to him?"

"Divine retribution."

"Wait, you're telling me they were Gods?"

"Yes."

"But they looked like you!"

Pock and Cock smiled at Dove, "We know, they're our…"

"No, don't tell me…"

"…Brothers."

Dove shook his head and walked back into The Doves Head Inn to get a brush to sweep away the ashes.

Tales from Ashen Falls

About the Author

Paul Lavender was born in Gateshead in the north-east of England in 1968. He now lives in Worcester in the West Midlands. He is still a supporter of Gateshead F.C though!

He is married and has a son.

In his working life, he has been an Electrician and a Manager for a logistics company but is currently a stay at home dad.

The Eighth God is his first novel; the second will be called The Sect of Seven, and the third will be Helekose. Paul expects the series to run into eight books, but you never can tell with these things!
If you're looking for The Eighth God, you can sometimes find him on an Xbox!

If you have any comments - good or bad - you can reach me on Twitter at @paullavender6, but please no trolls as they won't make an appearance until book 5!

Printed in Poland
by Amazon Fulfillment
Poland Sp. z o.o., Wrocław